THE
FISH WHO FOUND
THE SEA

Dedicated to children of all ages

Sounds True
Boulder, CO 80306

Published 2020

Book design by Ranée Kahler

Printed in South Korea

Library of Congress Cataloging-in-Publication Data

Names: Watts, Alan, 1915-1973. author. | Le, Khoa, 1982- illustrator.
Title: The fish who found the sea / by Alan Watts ; illustrated by Khoa Le.

Description: Boulder : Sounds True, Inc., 2020. | Audience: Ages 4-8
Identifiers: LCCN 2019034961 (print) | LCCN 2019034962 (ebook) |
  ISBN 9781683642893 (hardback) | ISBN 9781683642909 (ebook)
Subjects: LCSH: Philosophy, American—20th century—Juvenile literature. |
  Philosophy and religion—Juvenile literature.
Classification: LCC B945.W323 F57 2020 (print) | LCC B945.W323 (ebook) |
  DDC 191—dc23
LC record available at https://lccn.loc.gov/2019034961
LC ebook record available at https://lccn.loc.gov/2019034962

10 9 8 7 6 5 4 3 2 1

THE FISH WHO FOUND THE SEA

BY ALAN WATTS

ILLUSTRATED BY
KHOA LE

sounds true
BOULDER, COLORADO

Once upon a time, there was a fish
who lived in the Great Sea.
And because he was just an ordinary fish
who had never known anything outside
the Great Sea, he was not really
aware that he was in it.

He swam up and down and around, without ever
noticing that he was moving through the water.
For the water was transparent. Wherever he
moved, it got out of the way of his nose, and yet
gave him something against which he could push
with his tail and so move himself along.

Without it he could neither swim nor live,
but, for all he knew, he might just as well
have been moving in empty space.

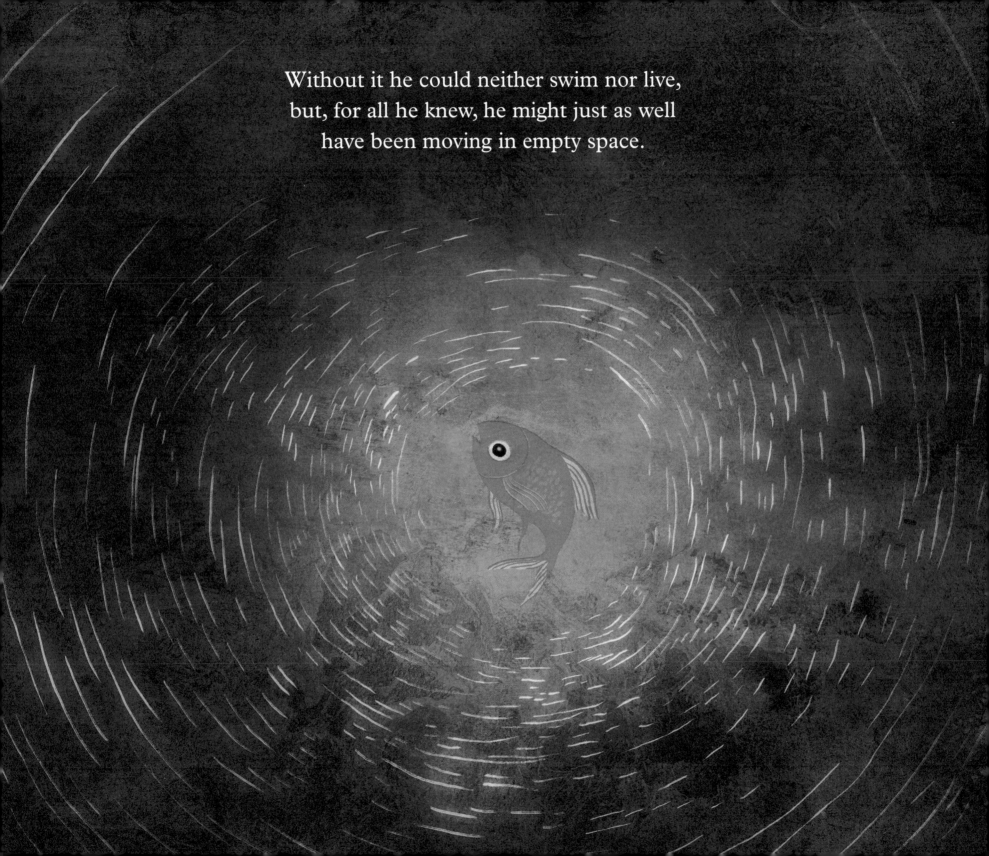

Then one day something peculiar happened to
him. He began to think how curious it was
that he could swim, for here he was moving
up and down and around in the midst of
nothing at all, and all by his own power.

This, he thought, was surely very clever of himself.

And then something else happened. You know
how it is when you start thinking about something
you do automatically, such as breathing
or riding a bike: you begin to get confused.

It was the same with this fish.

He began to get confused in his swimming. Looking down into waters below him, he was suddenly terrified at the thought that he might forget how to swim altogether and go plunging forever into the darkness.

At that moment all his skill
at swimming left him, and
he began to fall.

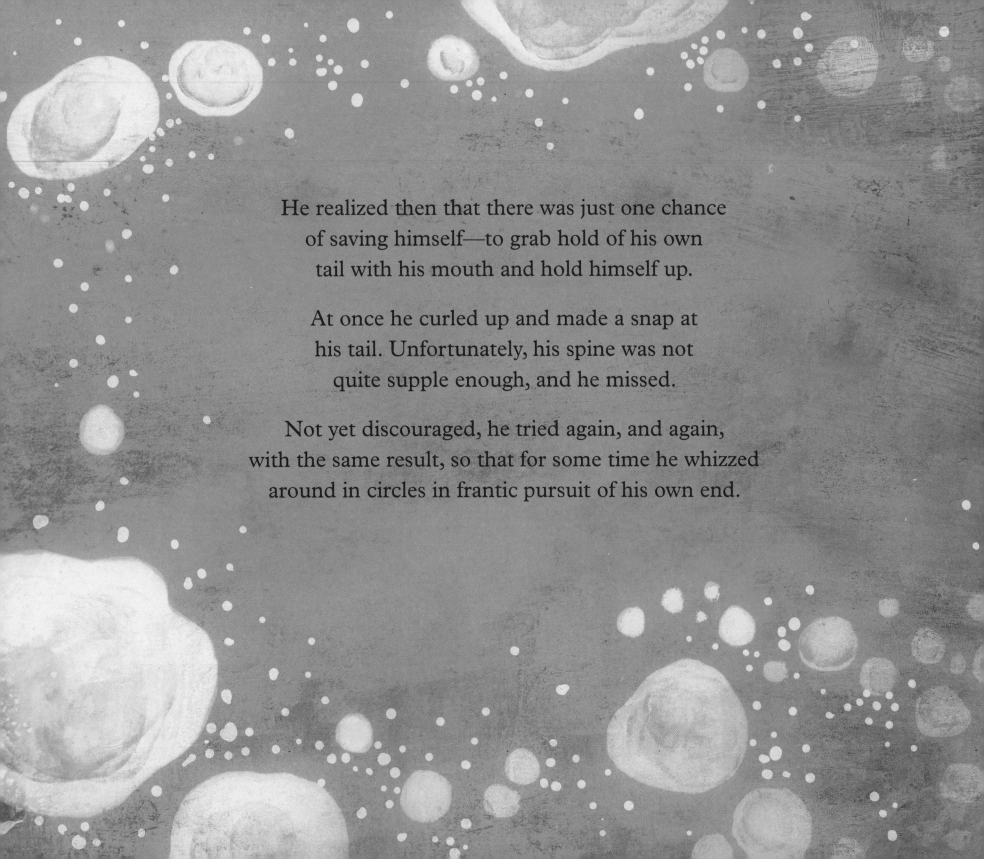

He realized then that there was just one chance
of saving himself—to grab hold of his own
tail with his mouth and hold himself up.

At once he curled up and made a snap at
his tail. Unfortunately, his spine was not
quite supple enough, and he missed.

Not yet discouraged, he tried again, and again,
with the same result, so that for some time he whizzed
around in circles in frantic pursuit of his own end.

The faster he chased his tail, the faster it moved away. This had been going on for some time when he began to realize that he was not getting anywhere, that his life was becoming dull, meaningless, and horribly monotonous.

But he was much too
frightened to stop.

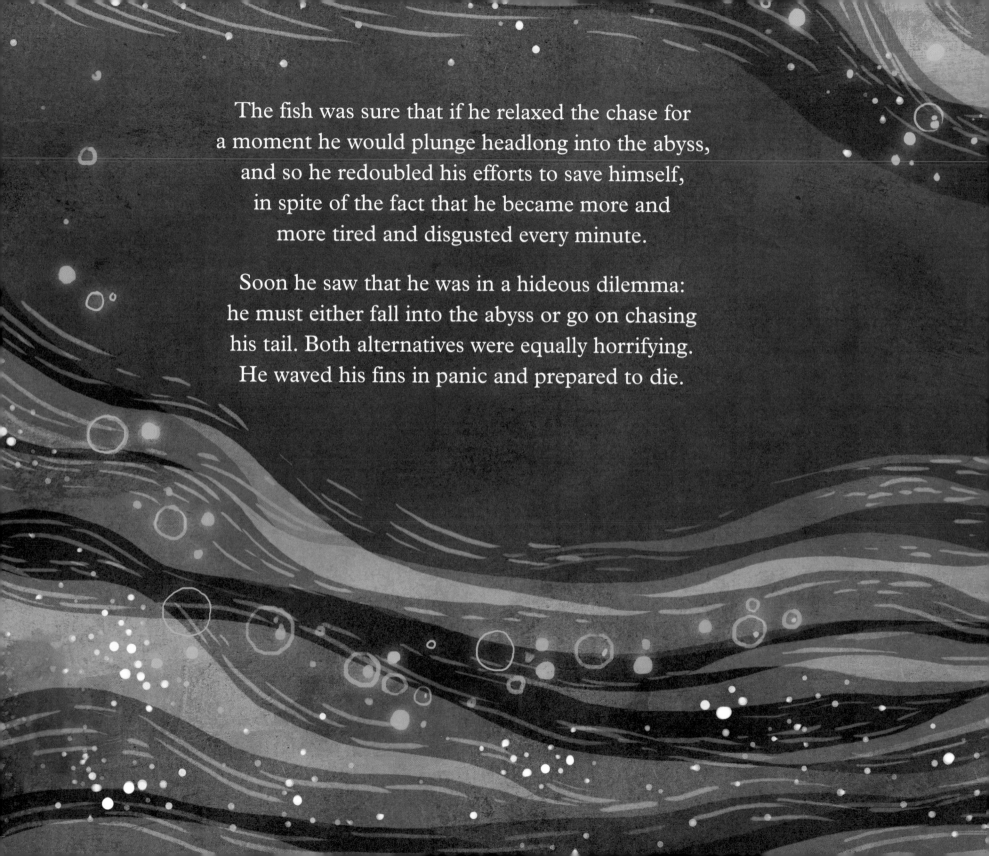

The fish was sure that if he relaxed the chase for
a moment he would plunge headlong into the abyss,
and so he redoubled his efforts to save himself,
in spite of the fact that he became more and
more tired and disgusted every minute.

Soon he saw that he was in a hideous dilemma:
he must either fall into the abyss or go on chasing
his tail. Both alternatives were equally horrifying.
He waved his fins in panic and prepared to die.

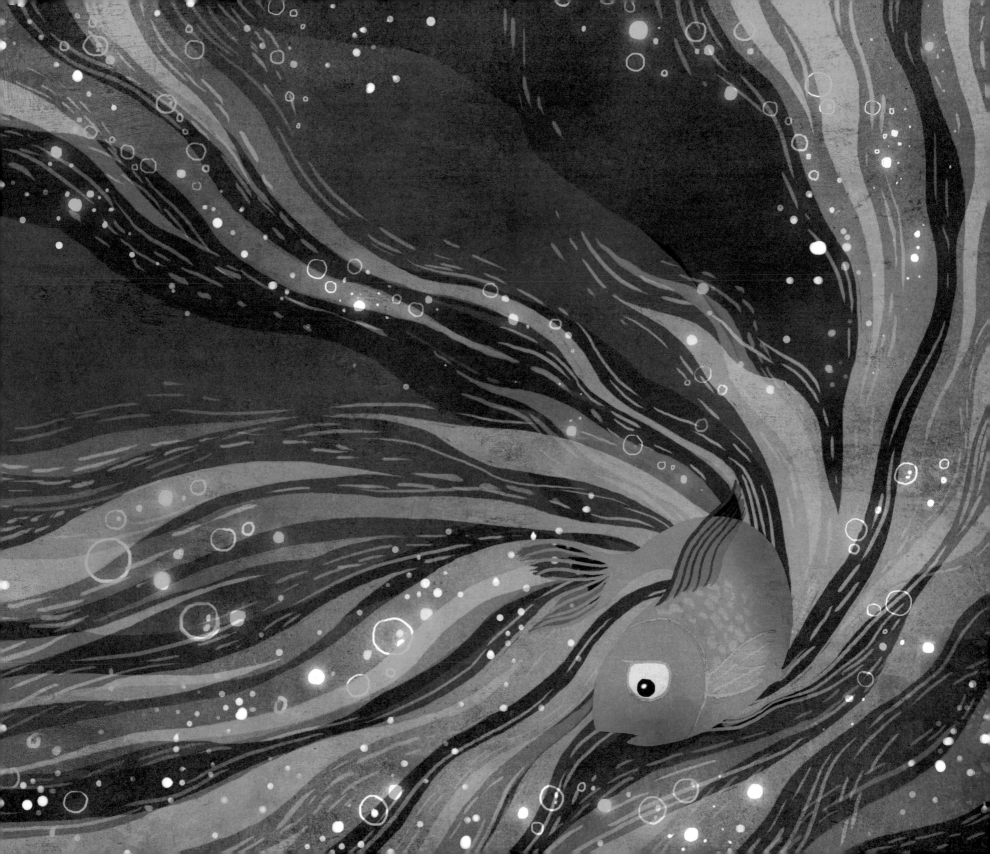

In the meantime, the Great Sea had been watching
this extraordinary behavior with mixed feelings
of amusement and sorrow.

For the Great Sea was as loving as it was vast. It gave all
the creatures of the deep room to live and swim around.
It never intruded upon them, always retiring generously
before their noses and letting itself be pushed by
their tails so that they could move along.

Still more, the Great Sea always surrounded them in
such a way that it bore them up, and made itself transparent
so that they could see where they were going and enjoy
all the wonders of the deep.

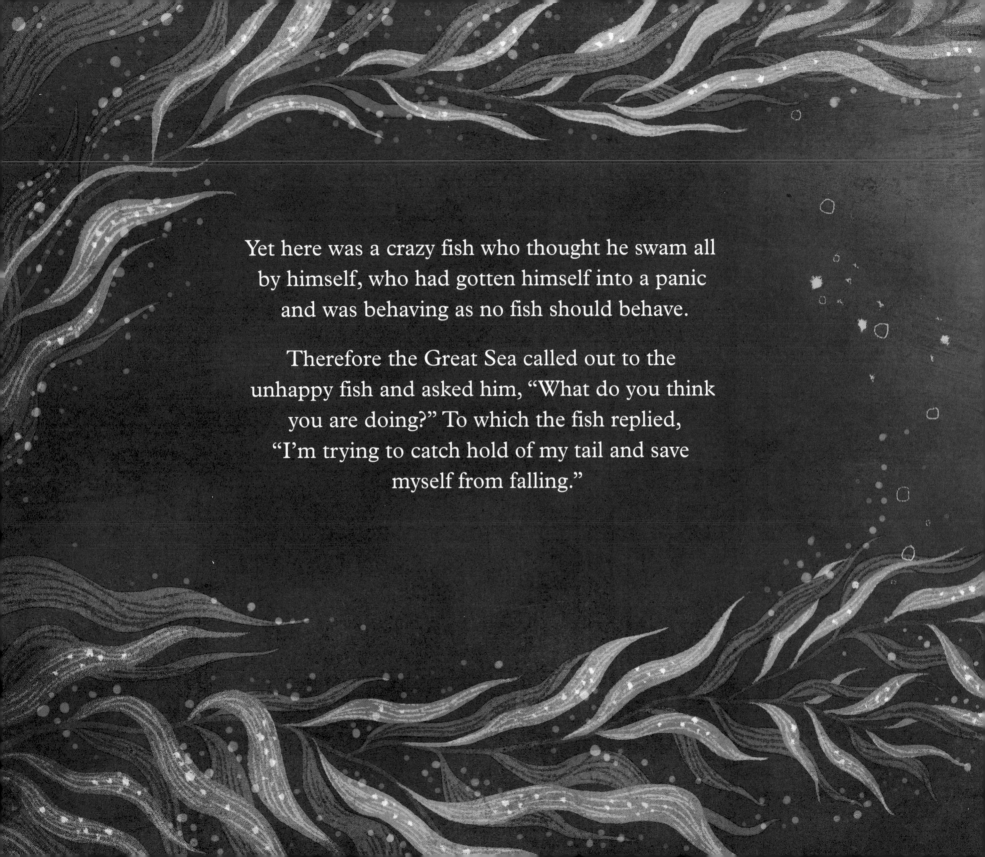

Yet here was a crazy fish who thought he swam all
by himself, who had gotten himself into a panic
and was behaving as no fish should behave.

Therefore the Great Sea called out to the
unhappy fish and asked him, "What do you think
you are doing?" To which the fish replied,
"I'm trying to catch hold of my tail and save
myself from falling."

"You have been doing that for a long time," observed the Great Sea, "and you are no nearer to catching it than when you started. So why haven't you fallen yet?"

"Don't bother me!" retorted the fish. "Can't you see I'm busy?"

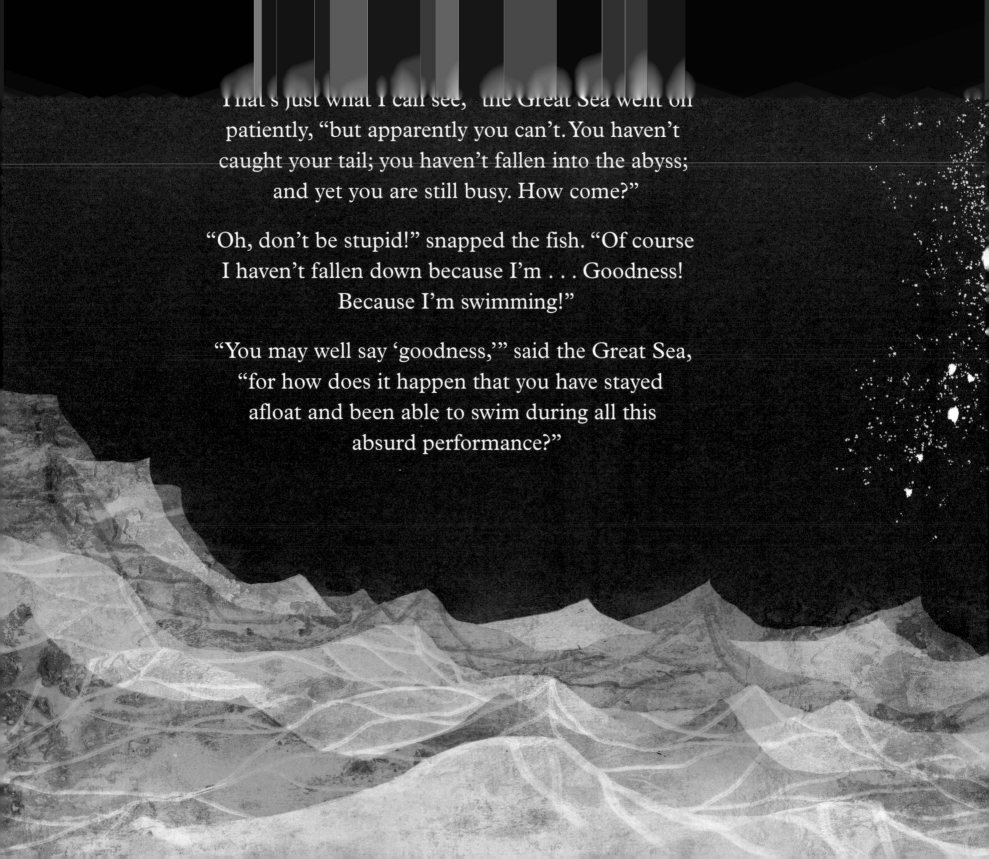

That's just what I can see," the Great Sea went on patiently, "but apparently you can't. You haven't caught your tail; you haven't fallen into the abyss; and yet you are still busy. How come?"

"Oh, don't be stupid!" snapped the fish. "Of course I haven't fallen down because I'm . . . Goodness! Because I'm swimming!"

"You may well say 'goodness,'" said the Great Sea, "for how does it happen that you have stayed afloat and been able to swim during all this absurd performance?"

There was no one to be seen, and . . . It was
strange, but although he wasn't doing anything
himself, he was still floating in the water, though
it seemed to him as if he were suspended in
empty space by some invisible force.

"There now," continued the Great Sea, "you thought you were doing it all by yourself, and you never knew that I hold you up all the time. I have given all of myself to you, and yet you have forgotten me and wasted yourself in pursuing your own end. For it is in me that you live and swim and are able to be a fish, and to you I have given the height and the depth, the length and the breadth of myself in which to swim."

From that moment, the fish was happier
than any other fish in all the waters of
the world. Setting his own end behind him,
where it belonged, he set out to explore
the ends of the Sea.

And he found that whether he moved up or down, to the left or to the right, everywhere the Great Sea expanded before him and supported him, so much so that he swooped and climbed and danced in joy—a creature in his true element, out of himself and into the Sea, where, indeed, he had been all the time.

As little girls, our father Alan Watts often regaled us with imaginative stories, limericks, and nonsense poems. *The Fish Who Found the Sea* is one such story. He wrote this parable in the mid-1940's when he was an Anglican priest and a chaplain at Northwestern University. Originally published in the *Holy Cross Magazine* in September 1944, it appeared three decades later in a couple of youth periodicals under the title *The Fish and the Great Sea* and was also included in the book *Cloud-Hidden, Whereabouts Unknown* in the essay "Spectrum of Love" (Pantheon, 1973). We hope you enjoy this picture book edition, the first of its kind. May you, like the little fish, dance always in the joy of your true element.

Joan and Anne Watts

This was too much for the fish. He
stopped his chase and looked around
to see who was talking to him.